W9-AHH-040

DISCARD

PRINCESSES
ARE PEOPLE, TOO

TWO * MODERN * FAIRY * TALES

PRINCESSES
ARE PEOPLE, TOO

TWO * MODERN   FAIRY * TALES

Susie Morgenstern

illustrated by **Serge Bloch**

VIKING

VIKING
Published by the Penguin Group
Penguin Putnam Books for Young Readers, 345 Hudson Street,
New York, New York 10014, U.S.A.
Penguin Books Ltd, Registered Offices: Harmondsworth, Middlesex, England

First published in France as *Même les princesses doivent aller à l'école*, 1991, and
Un jour mon prince grattera, 1992, by l'école des loisirs.
This edition published in 2002 by Viking,
a division of Penguin Putnam Books for Young Readers

1 3 5 7 9 10 8 6 4 2

Text copyright © 1'école des loisirs, 1991, 1992
Translation by Bill May, copyright © Penguin Putnam Inc., 2002
Illustrations copyright © Serge Bloch , 2002
All rights reserved

LIBRARY OF CONGRESS CATALOGING-IN-PUBLICATION DATA
Morgenstern, Susie Hoch.
[Meme les princesses doivent aller a l'école. English]
Princesses are people too : two modern fairy tales / by Susie Morgenstern ;
illustrations by Serge Bloch ; translated by Bill May.
p. cm.
Summary: In the first story, Princess Yona and her parents slowly adapt to a
world in which people seem to think that royalty belong only in books. In the
second, Princess Emma doesn't care how handsome or rich a prince is, if only he
can scratch her back until the terrible itch stops.
ISBN 0-670-03567-X (hardcover)
[1. Princesses—Fiction. 2. Fairy tales.] I. Bloch, Serge ; ill. II. May, Bill.
III. Morgenstern, Susie Hoch. Un jour mon prince grattera.
English. IV. Title.
PZ8.M8245 Pr 2002   [Fic]—dc21   2001006306

Printed in U.S.A.
Set in Stempel Schneidler, Greymantle, Weehah
Book design by Teresa Kietlinski

For Princess Ariana
and Princess Talia
and their Bubie Shaindel

PRAISE FOR
A Book of Coupons

"With the same ineffable sweetness she displayed in *Secret Letters from 0 to 10* (1998), Morgenstern offers another offbeat tale. There's a great tenderness in Morgenstern's treatment of the elderly teacher, his students, and even the prickly principal. Serge Bloch's sketches are just right." —*Booklist*

"Morgenstern's witty and poignant tribute to great teachers everywhere proclaims what education should be about. The real gift this Santa gives his students is a love for learning." —*The Horn Book*

PRAISE FOR
Secret Letters from 0 to 10

★ "Wrought with energy and wit, this chronicle of Ernest's metamorphosis from sheltered naïf into vibrant young man is not to be missed."
—*Publishers Weekly*, starred review

♦ "Certain to enchant readers. A novel to cherish."
—*Kirkus*, pointer review

CONTENTS

Even Princesses
Have to Go to School

THINGS were not going well for Princess Yona and her parents. There just weren't many royal families around anymore. It seemed like they were living in a land where people thought of kings and royalty as something that only belonged in books.

Their castle had fallen into ruins. When it rained, the royal family had to use their left hands to eat and their right hands to hold umbrellas over their heads, because there wasn't any money left to repair the leaky roof. Well, it could have been worse. After all, it's not that hard to eat macaroni with one hand.

All of their servants and employees were long gone; there were no valets, no cooks, no governesses, and no gardeners. The last to be sent away had been the princess's tutors, who had come each day to give her lessons in Latin, Greek, French, German, Russian, and Italian. With tears in their eyes, they had told her, each in turn: Vale! χαίρε, Au revoir, Auf Wiedersehen, до свидания, and Arrivederci.

Princess Yona's life wasn't much fun. Her father, King George CXIV, paced back and forth all day long—he averaged about ten thousand paces per hour. He scrunched his eyebrows, furrowed his brow, cleared his royal throat, and said at least eighty times a day to his only daughter, "Don't forget that you're a princess!"

Her mother, Queen Fortuna, wasn't nearly as active as her father. She stayed in bed practically all day under her enormous patched eiderdown covers. Whenever Princess Yona came to see her, she groaned, "Above all, don't forget that you're a princess!"

The princess wasn't likely to forget this detail. It was all she ever thought about. She never had anything to do. Bored. Bored out of her wits. Bored, bored, and bored. She was pretty sure being a princess was what was making her so bored and lonely. Her father looked hurt when she answered, "Sure, I'm a princess, but what good is that?" He didn't say anything and just kept pacing all over the castle.

Since her tutors had left, she'd had absolutely nothing to do, except try to avoid her father and mother, and try to keep her toes from freezing in the drafty castle. She didn't have any friends—she'd never even learned the word "friend" in any language. "Sports," "fun," and "laugh" were also unfamiliar words. Even though there was a TV in the castle, it had been broken for as long as she could remember. She had nothing to do but invent games to play with herself: she made up strange stories; she imagined living on another planet; she dreamed of being a princess in a real kingdom, in a renovated castle, with a smiling prince, far, far from her poor parents. Sometimes she jumped with her frayed jump rope and sang sad rhymes: "Oh my, oh dear, oh lord! Why am I so terribly bored?" Or with a broken bit of charcoal, she might draw a mural. With a pack of old playing cards, she played some lonely games or tried to predict a happier future than her present.

The only visitors the family ever had were bill collectors. But then one day a couple pulled up in a Rolls-Royce. They took one look at the castle and bought it on the spot.

Yona couldn't believe their luck. She'd had quite enough of each of the fifty-seven rooms of this ancient, gigantic castle. When they arrived in their new palace, she was in seventh heaven. It was a four-room apartment—complete with a modern kitchen and bathroom. Hot and cold water flooded

out of the faucets. She flushed the toilet just to hear the beautiful new music.

But the best part was their noisy neighbors. They could be heard shouting and playing all the time through the apartment's paper-thin walls. Yona could practically follow an entire television show one of her neighbors was watching. She listened to a couple fighting downstairs and to some people dancing upstairs.

From the balcony, Yona could see signs of life everywhere: the underwear and socks of her neighbors hanging on laundry lines, cars speeding past. She could even see into the apartments across the street and watch people having their breakfast. So far, the only trouble with the new palace was that she crossed paths with her parents a thousand times a day. And every time she saw them, the only thing they said to her was "Don't forget that you're a princess!"

Still, between watching the traffic on their busy street and listening to the noises in the building, Yona wasn't as lonely or as bored as she had been. With all of these people around she knew she would meet someone. But there was one problem. Every one of her neighbors left in the morning and didn't come back until the end of the day. Only the king, queen, and princess stayed at home, which made the days very long.

She was especially sad that the young neighbors left every day. Where were all of these kids going, all bundled up in their coats and carrying strange packs on their backs? They left at the same time each day for some mysterious destination. Wherever it was, the princess decided she wanted to go, too.

Sometimes the king and queen allowed

Yona to leave the apartment to pick up some milk or a can of sardines or some bread. Of course they always told her, "Don't forget that you're a princess." One day the princess decided to take advantage of one of these outings, and followed a group of kids on their mysterious journey. Eventually they came to the entrance of a huge, rundown building that had a tall fence around it. Yona would have traded her crown for a chance to join them in the playground where they jumped, ran, and yelled. Then suddenly, as if by magic, they formed several neat lines and followed a grown-up inside. From her hiding place behind a bush, she saw them all disappear. She was so jealous. *They* got to have fun together in this giant cement palace, while she had nothing to do with herself except remember that she was a princess.

She followed the children every day.

Her jealousy grew. Why should she have to suffer so much just because she was a princess? She didn't think these kids looked much different from her. She had to admit that no one else had a big fluffy dress with a long, flowing train, but Yona was used to her clothes. She thought it was entirely normal to wear fancy dresses because she was, after all—don't forget—a princess.

While she watched them turn somersaults

and trip each other, she daydreamed about joining them. One lovely Thursday, a little girl in the courtyard happened to see her. At first the little girl couldn't believe her eyes. She moved closer to the fence to make sure she wasn't imagining things. "Why are you standing there?" she asked.

"I'm watching you."

"How old are you?"

"Eight."

"Why don't you go to school?"

"Because I'm a princess—I think."

"I can see that," said the girl, exasperated, "but I think even princesses have to go to school.

At this extraordinary statement, a huge

and hopeful smile spread across Yona's face. "How do I go to school?"

"You don't need to do anything except show up. Come on!"

But the gate was locked and there was no way for her to climb over it with her long dress and train. Big tears began to splash down the princess's cheeks.

"What are you crying for? Don't be a dork! All you have to do is come back tomorrow at eight A.M."

Yona stopped crying and happily went on her way. "Dork"—what a beautiful word! She'd never heard it before. "I'm two things: a princess and a dork." She was ecstatic that she wasn't just a princess anymore.

That night, Yona forgot to set her alarm clock and she woke up around ten the next morning. When she finally got to the front gate, it was closed and locked. The little girl from the day before told her: "What a nerd you are! I *told* you eight o'clock."

The princess left, only a little disappointed. "I'm a princess, it's true, but also a dork and a nerd. I'll come back tomorrow."

The next morning, she sprang from her bed at dawn so she wouldn't be a second late. She tiptoed out of the apartment hours before the king and queen would wake up. But this time when she got to the mysterious building and stood in front of the gate, she didn't see a single person anywhere. No kids, no adults. Yona felt abandoned. She stood there for a few minutes until someone walked by and told her, "Today is Saturday. School's closed for the weekend."

She returned home with warm croissants for her royal parents and waited for Monday to come.

On Monday she arrived early again, before anyone else. When the kids got to school, she slipped into the courtyard with them, trying to seem inconspicuous—which is tough when you're wearing a long skirt and a crown. Curiously, no one said a thing as she lined up with the rest of them.

She lowered her eyes, trying hard to make herself invisible, and followed the person in front of her.

She made it all the way to the door before a lady stopped her. "What are *you* doing here? *You're* not in my class!"

"I want to come in too, Madame, please."

"Do you live around here?"

"Yes—we just moved here."

"Well, your parents must come and enroll you. We must have all of the paperwork."

Yona left again, discouraged, but determined

to make her father come see this woman. She knew this was going to be hard. Her father never left the apartment for anything.

Yona ran into the apartment practically screaming. "Papa, you have to come sign me up this afternoon."

"Where do you want to be signed up, my adored princess?"

"The place that all the kids go every day."

"Where is that?"

"I think it's called 'school.' All of them go, with big packs on their backs. They play and then they go into a palace where they spend the day having fun."

"School! That's not for you! That's not for a princess!"

"Please, Papa. They have so much fun there

and it's not fair. I'm jealous. I want to go."

"No. It can't be. Period. That's it."

The princess tried everything she could think of to convince her father, but she didn't have any luck. Finally she was forced to use her most powerful weapon—she threw a tantrum, complete with screaming, crying, and even some rolling on the floor.

Like all good fathers, King George wanted to make his daughter happy, even if it went a bit against his principles. So, although he was only half convinced, he took off his royal slippers and robe, got dressed, and walked royally to the school.

When they turned the corner and the king saw the building, he stopped in his tracks.

"Hurry up, Papa! What's the problem?"

"No, it's not possible! This place is too ordinary! It isn't for a princess!"

"You have all the papers, though, right?"

"Yes."

"Come on." She grabbed his hand, as if he were just a dog on a leash.

When they walked in, King George was pale, but he cleared his royal throat and announced to the principal, "I've come to enroll my daughter, the princess Yona."

"Very good, sir," said the principal. "I assume you have the proper papers?" King George grudgingly handed over Yona's royal birth certificate and the royal gas and electric bill.

All the principal said was "Hrumph" as she registered the name of Princess Yona in the school records.

❧

Yona dressed in her usual princess fashion for her first day of school. She didn't want to, particularly, but she didn't have anything in her closet except for long skirts and gowns. She also kept her crown sitting royally on her head. It had been given to her when she was born, and she only took it off to wash her hair.

Before saying good-bye, her father and mother stood looking at her like it was the end of the world. They said to her in a sad chorus, "Don't forget that you're a princess. . . ."

When she arrived, the little girl who had so nicely told her she was a dork and a nerd invited her to play.

"What's your name?"

"Yona. You?"

"Laura. Want to race?"

Laura began to run. Yona tried to follow, but she tripped on her train, which tore a little. While she was inspecting the tear, a boy suddenly lifted up her flowing skirt and hid himself under her royal dress.

She didn't want to be impolite, but she wasn't really happy having a boy hiding under her skirt. Laura quickly came to her rescue and chased him out. To thank her, Yona let Laura try on her crown.

As long as she was sitting at her desk doing the work her teacher assigned, everything went fine. It was just when she got up and her huge skirts got tangled and caught on people's feet that she remembered she was a princess and there was nothing she could do about it. One day, when the teacher tripped on her billowing skirt, the whole class laughed their heads off, and she gave Yona a really royal dirty look. Another day some boys stole her crown and threw it in the air like a football.

After school one day Laura blurted out, "Why do you always wear that costume?"

"It's not a costume. I'm a princess."

Laura's father was waiting for her in his car in front of the school. He honked and yelled to his daughter, "How's my princess?"

For Yona, this was a big surprise. "Do you mean you're a princess, too?"

"You're really a dork! Of course I'm a princess. All little girls are princesses in their father's eyes."

Yona was so relieved by this news. Suddenly she didn't feel like she was the only princess in the world anymore.

"So, when you leave for school, your father also says, 'Don't forget that you're a princess,'" she asked.

"No, he says, 'Good-bye, my princess.'"

❧

Yona's return home from school always caused a lot of drama. Her beautiful gowns were always torn, her shawl was covered in mud, and her shoes were stained. She didn't look like a princess at all.

And every day her mother said, "You can't go back to that place! It's no place for a princess!"

Finally, one day Yona said, "Well, actually my class is full of princesses."

"That's ridiculous! What are you talking about?"

"It's true, Laura told me, and I heard her father calling her 'my princess.'"

"They have no respect for bona fide royalty!" continued her mother, not listening.

"That's not true, Mother. Now get out of bed. You have to take me to get some tennis shoes. I can't run in these silk slippers."

Queen Fortuna was so surprised at her daughter's command that she couldn't think of anything else to do but listen. She left her royal bed and took Yona to the mall to buy a pair of tennis shoes. "Thank goodness no one will be able to see these under your long skirt," the queen said. "But they do look comfortable," she added, sighing almost jealously. And then, while Yona was looking at some socks, the queen hid in a corner and tried on a pair for herself. She bought them quickly, without her daughter seeing.

Yona's mother began accepting little by

little that it just wasn't practical for Yona to dress like a princess for school. She started buying her jeans, sweaters, socks, and all kinds of non-princess clothes. Queen Fortuna actually began to enjoy strolling around the mall, and convinced her husband to come along with her. They found so many beautiful things to buy that King George began to think he might want to get his first job. That way he could earn money to buy some kingly and queenly jeans, too.

Yona made a lot of friends at school, and she often brought them home in the afternoons. Her mother didn't stay in bed all day long anymore. In fact, she spent the day making fancy treats such as royal muffins and Queen Fortuna Napoleons. Her father became an active member of the PTA and helped plan renovations for the front of the school and the cafeteria. It was even his idea to put a moat around the school. He also found a great job in a company that he liked very much. And he bought a television. He still said "Don't forget you're a princess" to Yona out of habit, but sometimes he even had trouble remembering that he was a king.

Everyone might have forgotten that Yona was a princess if it weren't for the little crown that she wore every day, like it was stuck to her head. Mostly Yona didn't think about it. It was just like her hair, her skin, or her ears. Eventually, the other kids in her class stopped noticing it, too. But sometimes, when it made her head itch, she remembered her crown was there and was reminded that she was first—and most importantly—a person, and then, after all, who can deny it, a princess.

END

Someday
My Prince
Will Scratch

PRINCESS Emma lay back, snuggled into an enormous pillow, and propped her feet up. She sighed contentedly. "In bed with a book. This is the life!"

She was reading a story about a brave, handsome prince and his quest to rescue a princess. She had read so many stories like this that they had all begun to blur together. These princes were courageous, handsome and, truth be told . . . all the same. They never tired of killing the most ferocious dragons, the most monstrous bandits, of crossing the hottest seas of fire. Each of them was *the* best. And of course each of them wanted a beautiful princess for his reward.

And Emma was exactly that—a beautiful princess, or almost. She sighed again. All she had to do was sit and wait . . . with a book. Only, she wasn't particularly attracted to these vain princes who reached for the sun, the moon, and the stars. She preferred reading their stories to actually meeting them and being forced to say, "Good evening. . . . Good to meet you. . . . How are you?"

No. She would rather stay in bed and leave the princes where they belonged—in a book.

Emma loved her bed. She loved lying there all by herself. Sometimes when she gazed through her window at the big, blue sky, she liked to pretend it had been put there for her and her alone. Such a beautiful blue sky. . . .

Princess Emma was about to release another enormous sigh of satisfaction when suddenly a familiar beast attacked her. A horrible monster with forty fingers and forty toes!

It always attacked her at the most unexpected moments, as if to prove that life will surprise you when you're least expecting it.

And now, again, the plague had struck!

She was completely overcome by painful itching—she felt like she had turned into one gigantic mosquito bite. She performed her octopus imitation, searching frantically with her too-short arms to find the exact spot that itched—right in the very center of her back. Her right hand couldn't find it, and her left hand never even came close. How do you find something that is not quite here and not quite there, a little higher, a little lower, more to the right, more to the left, a vicious little demon always running this way and that, until you finally just WANT TO SCREAM?!?!?

"Argh. Aaaaargh—oooooowwww!" Princess Emma cried in a panicked voice while scratching helplessly away.

Her mother immediately appeared by her side. "What's wrong, sweetheart?"

Princess Emma suddenly stopped midscratch and declared in a solemn tone, "I know exactly the kind of prince I want to marry."

"But, sweetheart, I've always known the type of prince you need: rich, handsome, coura-geous, powerful, and sole inheritor to a kingdom at least as great as our own."

"Forget about all of that!"

"You certainly can't expect anything less!"

But Princess Emma didn't care at all about royalty, riches, or even intelligence, if only this prince could accomplish the simple task she was thinking about.

"What I want," she said to her mother matter-of-factly, "is to find someone who can scratch my back in just the right spot until it finally stops itching!"

This made perfect sense to the princess. Whenever the horrible plague struck, the rest of the world vanished—except for that one appalling, exasperating, infuriating itch.

She was attacked again several weeks later, during the court ball, while she was dancing with a very adorable prince. It wasn't her knees trembling—only that impossible spot in the center of her back.

She led the prince toward the terrace and told him, "My handsome Prince Vance, this is your test and your only chance!" Then, in a haughty, royal voice, she declared, "Scratch my back!"

The prince, stunned, began to blush, choke, and splutter. He couldn't move and he had no idea what to do.

The princess twisted and contorted herself. "Hey—you don't have all night! Come on!"

At her insistence, he nervously stretched out his index finger to her shoulder, but only managed a light tickle, not anything you could call a scratch.

"Not like that! You have ten fingers for a reason! Use them!"

He made another half-hearted attempt, but the princess could hardly feel a thing.

Princess Emma quickly realized that she couldn't expect much from this timid tickler.

"This is the end of your dance, Vance!"

She found refuge in a corner of the palace and rubbed her back against the rough stones.

The tremors subsided but a light itch remained.

Without another word she returned to her bed with a book.

Another prince soon arrived, interrupting her reading, to take her to dinner. It was the brilliant Prince Igor. He was telling her all about school and professors when the itch struck again.

"Scratch my back!" she shrieked.

"Wait a minute," said the prince. "Let's examine the problem scientifically and methodically."

"Scratch, Igor!"

"Okay. Turn around."

She turned her back to him gratefully, but she got no relief. She turned back to find the prince making a sketch of her back on a paper napkin.

"It can't wait anymore, Igor! Scratch!" she screamed.

"I'm just drawing a map to establish the precise geography of the area."

"Forget the geography and scratch my back!"

"Well, I need this map to find the precise place where the problem lies."

But the itch was getting more intense, moving back and forth, like an angry snake.

"Is it toward the north or the south? The east or the west?"

"Oh, why don't you just take your map and

go on a trip to the North Pole!" shrieked the agitated princess. She muttered under her breath, "You ask a simple favor that anybody with one hand could do for you, and what do you get? A map!"

Emma had to put a stop to this parade of pathetic princes. She needed to rest for a few weeks after seeing them.

೧౿

One day, she found herself in the company of a talkative prince who was a poet. Prince Drake explained to her at length how brave he was and all the miraculous things he had done since birth. Once, he bragged, he had recited a poem to an audience of ten thousand people. Emma was barely listening to him when all of a sudden the itch began to pull this way and that way under her skin.

"Hurry! Help!" she cried. "Scratch my back!"

"Hold on! Hold on!" he protested, standing

perfectly still in the park, looking like a statue of
William Shakespeare himself.

She stood, stunned, watching him concen-
trate, when suddenly he yelled, "Words can be
very powerful. Let's try a poem!"

"Why don't you just scratch my back?"

He raised his eyes to the sky and began
to recite:

> *"In a split second something goes crack.*
> *It's a secret place right in your back.*
> *Suddenly, you're in a craze,*
> *Trapped, like being in a maze.*
> *You search for hands to save your skin*
> *From this awful, itchy, icky thing.*
> *But unsure hands don't seem to work,*
> *Which leaves poor you to scratch and jerk.*
> *There's no known cure and you won't wait*
> *So you use words to change your fate.*
> *But all you ever seem to write*
> *Is 'Scratch my back with all your might!'"*

Princess Emma decided she liked this prince poet. He understood her. She told him, laughing, "Then do it!"

"No. I don't want to. I don't like scratching backs. No way."

"Oh, go jump in a lake, Drake!"

And that was the end of the prince poet.

Princess Emma had seen enough princes by now to know that it wasn't going to be easy to find the prince of her dreams. She retreated sadly to her room, wondering if its friendly walls and comforting books were all she really needed. Almost immediately a horrible itch appeared between her shoulder blades. She ran to the palace kitchen and grabbed a long fork. She began to scratch, but the fork was sharp and pointy. It felt like she was stabbing her back instead of scratching it. The itch didn't stop.

Emma knew she had to give every prince a chance, so she accepted a date with an engineer prince.

He didn't exactly look like the princes in her books. Prince Pat was rather short, with big glasses that swallowed up his face.

Nevertheless, he was friendly and a good conversationalist, and he had long fingers that looked perfect for scratching backs.

The inevitable soon happened and the

princess once again gave her order. "Pat, scratch my back!"

The engineer prince ran off, saying before he disappeared, "Don't worry! Help is on its way!"

A long time later, he rang the doorbell and presented the princess with a machine that looked like something you'd find in a dentist's office.

"I'm going to give you a demonstration," announced the prince. "When I push this button and I turn this dial, a lever starts to work, which controls the movement that automatically releases the simulated fingers. . . ."

The explanation lasted a long time. So did the itch.

Emma didn't have the patience for this. "You're a rat, Pat!"

<hr/>

This all seemed to last thirty-five eternities— a countless line of princes, each more annoying than the last. The endless cycle depressed her.

But there's more to life than lying around in bed. And so, Emma agreed to meet Prince O'Neil. He was a great talker and very entertaining. He had eyes like ice and long black hair. He looked a little like a crow. When the evil itch struck again, Princess Emma thought that he would immediately spring into action.

"Could you, please, please, nicely and softly, scratch my back?"

"I could," he said, sitting back, "if I wanted to!"

"And do you want to?"

"Well . . . I want to if you want me to. I'll tell you what. You scratch my back, I'll scratch yours."

She stared hard at O'Neil. This was a businessman prince . . . and he meant business. She did, too. "Okay! Me first!"

"No, me first." He took a watch out of his pocket. "On your mark, get set, go!"

She held out her hand and let it drag lightly over his back.

"Not like that!" he cried. "On the skin!"

She slid her fingers under his shirt and felt lots

of bumps and pimples. His back was a real dermatological disaster.

"Ugh! It's too gross, O'Neil. I don't want to scratch your back. It's disgusting."

"You don't scratch, I don't scratch."

"You know, you're really a creep. There goes your deal, O'Neil!"

Princess Emma began to get really upset.

"Why is it I have two hands, ten fingers, and millions of brain cells, but I can't scratch my own back! Why aren't we born with three hands?"

The bad dates and dances and ten-minute romances continued as the weeks and months waltzed along.

A lawyer prince advised her to file a complaint against the itch.

A magician prince tried to cast a spell.

A doctor prince wanted to put her in the hospital.

Princes came, princes went, but the itch remained.

Princess Emma got even sadder. Sometimes she sat up in bed late at night and cried. "I don't want doctors, lawyers, or any of these fancy princes. All I want is a prince who knows how to scratch." She began to think

she would stay in bed and spend the rest of her life reading. When an itch attacked, she would just grit her teeth and toss and turn, waiting for it to end.

Emma read until her eyes turned red. She read until there was nothing left to read. So she stood up, dressed, and went to the bookstore. Soon Emma had such a big pile of books she could hardly see over them. On her way to the counter to pay, she nearly knocked over poor Prince Ray. His arms were filled with books, just like hers.

He looked her in the eyes and said, "You must

love books as much as I do! Now I think I'm in love."

"What if he says that to all the princesses?" wondered Emma. But this prince didn't seem half bad. He wasn't ugly or handsome, but had a nice enough face. He wasn't talkative or quiet, not the poetic or scientific type. He was just . . . right.

They paid for their books, left the bookstore, walked together, and talked. Soon, they were inseparable.

A few months after they met, they looked at each other one day and at the same time said, "Let's get married!" But the princess added, "There's just one small problem—I have to be scratched in the right way, Ray."

"Don't you worry, I'll scratch you!" he promised. And he immediately began scratching away. He scratched and scratched while she itched and itched.

Then Princess Emma stopped squirming for a second. "Maybe having him scratch my back is just as good as actually getting rid of the itch," she realized.

So if it happened that on dark winter nights or some sunny spring days, Ray's scratching didn't entirely get rid of her itch, Emma understood. Prince Ray might scratch with only one hand, but he did it with all his heart.

Sometimes the itches stopped. Sometimes they didn't. Life went on. And so they lived more or less happily ever after.

END